Supervillain of the Day

SUPERVILLAIN OF THE DAY 5

DREAMS AND SHADOWS

by Katie Lynn Daniels

Cover design by Jordan Miller
Interior formatting by Aubrey Hansen

Special thanks to Elizabeth Kirkwood for reading absolutely
everything I sent her, however meaningless; to Jordan Miller for his
brilliant cover designs; to Elsa for her meticulous editing an
invaluable assistance in revising; to Aubrey Hansen for helping
clueless me with formatting and never getting tired of reading these
books; and to E and Brendan for telling me not to be afraid of the
dark.

For more information regarding permissions, contact the publisher
by visiting the website: Books.ProvideYourOwn.com or by writing to
the address below. For more information on Creative Commons
Licensing visit creativecommons.org.

Published by:
Provide Your Own – Books
PO Box 748
Tompkinsville, KY 42167
Website: Books.ProvideYourOwn.com

Print Edition, September 2013
ISBN-13: 978-0615834238 (Provide Your Own - Books)
ISBN-10: 061583423X
Library of Congress Control Number: 2013910804

This is a work of fiction. Any similarities to real people, living or
dead, are merely coincidental.

For Eddy
Because even when you weren't there
I knew you cared

TABLE OF CONTENTS

A TIME TO LIVE

Floyd woke up with his skin on fire, his head exploding, and the unsettling feeling that the world had ended without him. He tried to sit up, and decided that was a bad idea, opting to lay still for the moment instead. He opened and closed his eyes several times, wondering why it made no difference in the darkness surrounding him.

The darkness was unsettling. It was thick, and heavy, like a stage curtain or a funeral shroud. He breathed it into his lungs and it choked him, seeping into—

He jerked away from the nightmare, and the sudden movement made his head throb. The unsettling feeling grew into a sort of panic; something was very, very wrong here.

But the thought slipped away quietly, like water emptying out of a cracked vase. It went and left him drained, still, waiting like smooth sand for the next wave to crash.

When it came, he sat up suddenly, gasping for breath, nearly crying out with the fear of it. His panic drove him to his feet in spite of the sudden vertigo that hit him, and he ran headlong into a wall he couldn't see, clawing for a way out, desperate to escape.

For a brief moment, cold rationality hit him like a breath of fresh air, and he knew he was being controlled, that his thoughts and feelings were not his own. But before he could process what exactly that meant, the ability to think was stripped away from him and he sank down against the wall, uncaring.

The third time should have been the most brutal. The unnatural sensation of panic should have reduced Floyd to a cowering puddle of fear in the corner, but the effect had already grown old. He snatched the fear neatly out of his brain and shoved it into a corner with all the other nasty things he tried to forget about. Out loud he said:

"Stop toying with me. It won't work."

And then suddenly he was alone in his own mind, in a dark room.

He scrambled to his feet, eager to explore his surroundings, and promptly fell down. He sprawled on the floor, swore at the ceiling, and remembered that his head hurt, his skin was on fire, and it felt like the world had ended without him.

Which probably meant that he'd been killed in some nasty fashion, slept his way back to life, and missed the ending of the world.

That would explain why it was dark, in any case.

Whoever was enjoying messing around in his head decided to try a new tactic. Instead of fear he was suddenly hit with an overwhelming feeling of...

Shame.

He remembered in vivid detail every instance where he had done something stupid, and stood in Adams' office being berated for it. He could remember exactly how it felt wishing he hadn't done it, because in the end the prank wasn't worth the scolding, and—

Floyd could also remember every time he'd pulled something off and gotten away with it, and those times had been worth the scoldings for the others. He laughed.

He could feel the displeasure of his tormentor like a tangible thing in the darkness, and it only fed his self-satisfaction. Standing more carefully this time, and prepared to fight off his physical weaknesses, he finally began to explore his surroundings.

The walls were smooth, cold, and definitely metallic. So was the floor. Circumventing the room, he determined that there was no discernible form of egress. There was probably a sliding panel opening only from the outside.

Completing his inspection, he sat down again and tried to process the information he'd accumulated. He'd been captured. He was in a metal box. Escape from the metal box was impossible. The metal box contained nothing besides himself. There were no sharp edges anywhere. His captor was some kind of telepath. Quite possibly his prison had been built specifically for him.

He had no memory of the events leading up to his capture.

It was the last bit that bothered him the most. Short-term memory loss was normal, especially after serious injury, but it didn't mean he had to like it. And he'd been awake for some time now—hadn't he? It was impossible to measure time in the box, in the dark, but between the time he'd taken to examine his surroundings and the distractions provided by his mysterious host, surely it had been an hour or two.

He cleared his mind for a moment and waited to see if his captor would make another assault. Nothing happened.

He pondered possible routes of escape. Nothing plausible came to mind.

Floyd got bored very quickly. When he was bored, he had a tendency to do things that could be considered stupid and were in fact quite idiotic.

"Is that all you've got?" he shouted to the unseen entity that held him captive. "I mean, really. You're the first supervillain to successfully capture and imprison me, and that's all you planned to do to me?"

His voice echoed off the metal walls and rang loudly in his ears, and when the echoes faded, there was no reply.

"I mean really, it's a bit insulting," he continued rashly. "Where are the threats? The evil laughter? The crowd of snarling henchmen all bowing to your genius? Where are all the demands and instruments of torture?"

The fear was like a howling wind that twisted around him like a tornado, and squeezed until he couldn't breathe, until his blood froze in his veins. It was like every nightmare he'd ever had, relived in vivid, waking detail. It was like every time he'd died, afraid he would never wake up.

Then it was gone, leaving him weak and shaking, and as he pulled himself to his knees, he whispered:

"That was stupid."

Hollow laughter rang in his ears. It was impossible to determine where it was coming from. He knew only that it wasn't his own.

Before he had time to collect his thoughts, he was jerked away. Away from the prison cell, away from his own body. He was standing in a last desperate stand against the supervillains, and he was watching Joseph Adams die.

....

Floyd hated waking up as a general rule, and this was definitely the worst example he'd had to live through. When the darkness of his mind resolved into the darkness of his cell, he had no idea where he was or what had happened. Reality and memory separated slowly, like soup. All desire to taunt the supervillain had drained away with the life-blood of his only friend.

He remembered now. He remembered, and the knowledge left him cold and empty and hopeless. There was no one to watch his back. There was no one to mount a rescue. There was no one to tell him to stop making stupid decisions. He was every bit as alone as he had been when he first came to this planet.

He wanted to be angry, but he was too exhausted to care. He was vaguely aware of the supervillain laughing at him again. He ignored it. He tried to think things through, to remind himself that he'd seen people die before, that he was himself a killer. It didn't do any good.

He wanted to stand and pace, but when he tried to sit up, a wave of dizziness hit him, and he gave up the idea.

He wanted to be free. He wanted something to kill. He wanted to make sense of everything that had happened to him. He wanted—

He swore into the darkness and covered his face with his hands because what he wanted was to talk to Joseph, and that was never going to happen.

He didn't know what to do with that information. He tried to think about it rationally and stopped himself, for there was nothing rational about losing your only friend on earth.

He had to get out of here. He forced himself to his feet and felt his way around the room, but long before he completed his inspection, he knew it was hopeless. There was no way out. His only chance of escape would be when the supervillain came to gloat, and if the villain never came, he would die here.

The despair that wriggled its way through his thoughts wasn't real. It whispered to him that all was lost, that he had nothing to live for, that there was no hope, and that he would die alone, in pain, and imprisoned, forgotten by the world outside. He had failed his friend, and there was no one else to come for him. He should give up now.

It wasn't real. He knew it wasn't real, but a part of him didn't care.

When the attack faded and left him to the mercy of his own emotions, he still didn't care. Wrapped in a thick cocoon of sullenness, he fell asleep.

A WORLD OF SUPERVILLAINS
August 26, 2013

Almost a year after the first supervillain outbreak it would seem that the world has adjusted well to their new neighbors. And yet many questions have yet to be answered. Where did the villains come from? Can anyone become a villain? Do you know when you're being transformed or do you just wake up one morning with superpowers?

A TIME TO DIE

It all began on a normal day, or as normal as a day could get with Floyd around. It had been nearly two months since he'd been hired as an official consultant for Scotland Yard. He had a badge that proclaimed him as such, and even his own desk in the corner of Adams' office. This desk was where everyone else in the building tossed the case files they didn't understand. Floyd spent most of his time dashing back and forth and making demands on department resources, and the rest of it he spent arguing with the Chief Inspector about something he called "Emergency Supervillain Measures."

"What you're proposing is martial law!" the Chief Inspector shouted.

"I don't care what you call it," Floyd said in exasperation. "What I'm proposing will protect London."

"Regardless of the danger, the citizens of this city still have the right to decide what is best for their own safety."

It was an old argument, and nobody paid any attention to it any more.

"They're making stupid decisions," Floyd persisted.

"It's their right to make stupid decisions," the Chief Inspector said in a tone of finality.

Adams took this as his cue to keep his new consultant from getting fired. "Floyd!" he shouted.

"Their right is getting them killed," Floyd persisted.

"That is also their right," said the Chief Inspector wearily.

"Floyd!" Adams repeated.

"What?" Floyd said in irritation, finally giving up on the argument. The Chief Inspector retreated to his own office in relief.

"You're going to clear your desk," Adams ordered. "And then we're going to lunch."

Floyd glanced at the desk. "There's only like... seven folders there," he said. "What's the big deal?"

"That's not where they go and you know it."

Floyd ignored them and grabbed his coat. "I'll work on it when we get back," he said.

Adams leaned against the door frame and folded his arms. "We're not going anywhere until you clean up," he ordered.

Floyd glanced at him, and knew he was telling the truth.

"Kate was right," he muttered. "You really are obsessed."

"You can call Kate and complain about me later," Adams told him.

Floyd rolled his eyes and sat down to look at the folders.

"Done, done, done," he said, tossing three of them on Adams' desk. The remaining four he stuck on the bottom of a tidy stack on the corner of the desk. "Aren't *you* going to clean off your desk now?" he taunted.

"I'll do it when we get back," Adams retorted. "Come on then."

"Hypocrite," Floyd muttered, following him out of the building. Adams ignored him.

"You really need to stop arguing with the Chief Inspector," he said warningly, once he felt ready to converse again.

"I'm entitled to my opinions," Floyd growled.

"Perhaps," Adams said. "But you're not entitled to be constantly shouting them at your superior."

"I'm right, though," Floyd said, glaring furiously at whatever nearby objects caught his attention. "You know I am."

"Actually, I agree with the Chief."

"You're kidding, right?" Floyd said in exasperation. "How can you agree with him? I'm *right*."

Adams sighed and shook his head. "Being right doesn't always mean you're in the right," he tried to explain. "It's one of those morality issues you seem to have such trouble with."

"Morality has no place in a world overrun by supervillains," Floyd said.

"On the contrary," Adams said. "When we're faced with this much evil, it's more important than ever to cling to what we know is right."

"But as I said to the Chief, your so-called moral rights are getting your people killed!"

"That's their decision," Adams said, "and we have no business interfering with it."

"Well, their decisions are getting in the way of me doing my job."

"It's not your city, Floyd," Adams pointed out. "It's not even your country. So do your job as best as you can, keep your head down, and leave the politics to the natives, okay?"

Floyd didn't answer as they reached their usual restaurant, sat at their usual table, and ordered their usual drinks.

"You know what I do," Floyd said finally.

"Yeah," Adams said, confused. "So?"

"So, if I can't work within the system, then I'll work outside of it. You know that. If I'm not allowed to meddle in politics, or if they go against me, then I'll ditch the system."

"You're doing good work here," Adams said pragmatically.

"But it's not what I was sent to do," Floyd pointed out.

"So?"

"So what if there are repercussions?"

Adams shrugged. "Who cares? You worry too much."

"I can't help but worry," Floyd muttered. "It's my life."

"I'm sorry."

"It's not your fault."

"Do you ever—" Adams broke off abruptly.

"What?" Floyd asked, cocking his head in curiosity.

"Nothing," Adams said, regretting saying anything at all.

"You'll never get away with that with me," Floyd warned.

"The people who sent you here," Adams said, giving in. "Do you think you can ever forgive them?"

Floyd shrugged. "I don't even know who I would be forgiving," he said. He kept his voice neutral, but Adams saw how his hands tightened around the fork he held.

"I should have—" he started to apologize, but Floyd interrupted without hearing him.

"I never met them," he said, his eyes blazing. "They locked me in an empty room with an annoying computer and they left me there and I never even *met them.*"

"All you have is just a name," Adams murmured.

"The Department of Supervillain Help and Relief Services." Floyd spoke the words with visible distaste.

"No wonder you distrust the system," Adams agreed.

"Bureaucrats are the same throughout the galaxy," Floyd said.

"Floyd," Adams said uncertainly.

"I don't want your sympathy," Floyd snapped.

"Where are you going?" Adams asked, as Floyd scraped his chair back and stood.

"I have work to do," Floyd said shortly.

"What work?" Adams asked in disbelief.

"I'll find some!" Floyd snapped in frustration. "Just leave me alone."

"I'm sorry," Adams repeated helplessly as his friend stormed out of the room.

....

Floyd didn't get far before he realized he had no idea where he was going. He didn't work for the London Star any more, and so "working" didn't just mean wandering around until something unusual jumped out at him. He worked for Scotland Yard now, which meant cases and procedure. It was more efficient but it was also more structured. Floyd hated structure.

He hesitated a moment, letting people more sure of their destination walk around him as though he wasn't there. Then he sighed and turned back. Better to just go back to Scotland Yard and do things properly.

Five minutes later, he stopped again. He was being followed.

It was impossible to prove the feeling by merely looking around. He was surrounded by people coming and going. And yet he couldn't deny the prickling sensation invoked by staring, malevolent eyes. Slowly he started out again, only to be distracted by a noise.

Glancing in the direction the noise had come from, he saw a narrow alley running between two buildings. A creature more animal then human crouched on the pavement, cackling.

"Hey you," Floyd shouted, starting for him. "What's going on?"

The creature laughed and started to hop away. Floyd pursued it. No sooner was he out of sight of the main street then he realized that he had made a very bad decision. There were no people here, only the laughing, staring, invisible eyes.

"All right!" he called to the empty street. "What do you want?"

For a moment there was no answer and he felt vaguely foolish. Then a shadow stepped out of the wall. A lizard grew, faster than you could blink. A hulking monster appeared on the roof above him. Floyd looked around—he was surrounded.

"Okay." He held up his hands. "You've got me. Now what do you want?"

The henchmen laughed. Their laughter was like a pack of hyenas, but infinitely more sinister. The lizard-boy squealed like a pig. The hulk sounded like Santa Clause. The shadow sounded like he was choking. More creatures crept out of their hiding places, some more human than others.

"All right," Floyd said appreciatively. "You all have... very nice laughs. Very well developed. Now what do you want?"

Their laughter changed tone, but it didn't quite become words. Floyd became frustrated. Dealing with henchmen could be very similar to dealing with children.

"Who do you work for?" he asked.

They took turns answering in their raspy, nasty, slinking, slimy, irritating, grating, obnoxious voices.

"I work for Snake Man," lizard-boy hissed.

"We work for the Cauldron Keeper," a pair of misshapen twins squeaked.

"Mushroom Man."

"Moonshine."

"Tax Collector."

"Vitriol."

Round and round, their answers chased each other and more of them came out into the open. Floyd began to get worried.

15

"What do you want?" he interrupted. They paused, recoiled, collected themselves.

"We want you." They hissed and laughed and the sound of their collective voices began to grate on his nerves.

"Henchmen never work alone," Floyd called, stating the obvious. "Someone sent you. You're clearly working together, but you have different masters, so tell me: what's really going on here? Who are you working for?"

They didn't laugh again, but they grinned and began to come closer.

Henchmen aren't a threat. Floyd repeated it over and over, like a mantra. *They aren't a threat, they aren't a threat, just treat them like children...*

"What do you want?" he repeated, trying to sound authoritative. "Who sent you?"

Their grins broadened and they came closer.

Floyd shook his head, wondering if this was all a bad dream. What he was seeing conflicted with everything he'd ever observed, or been told to observe, in the behaviour of henchmen.

"Who are you working for?"

"You're a threat. A danger. You must be eliminated."

They were all saying the same things, and coming steadily closer.

"A collective," Floyd stammered. They halted their approach momentarily. "You're working together," Floyd continued, suddenly alight with new information. "Like bees. You're communicating..."

He trailed off realizing the implications of this revelation.

The henchmen laughed in glee, and then they attacked.

....

Adams sat alone in the restaurant feeling guilty after Floyd left. He pondered going after him, decided that he should let him be alone for a while, but then changed his mind again. Finally, he gave up, knowing he wouldn't be able to focus until he made things right with his friend. Paying the check, he left the restaurant only to be confronted by a new problem—he had no idea where Floyd might have gone. He could have gone home, he could have gone back to Scotland Yard, or he could be running around the rooftops of London, or fighting with henchmen underground.

Adams abandoned the idea of apology and reconciliation and decided to go back to work himself. Halfway there, he paused, distracted by a noise that seemed out of place in the usual midday hubbub of the street. It was a sort of snickering snarling noise that reminded him of... henchmen. He glanced down the narrow alley between two buildings, and made the decision to pursue the noise.

The last few henchmen saw him coming and beat a hasty retreat. Adams knew before he saw; he knew who they were pawing over like vultures fighting over a carcass.

"Floyd," he gasped, running the last few steps. "Floyd what happened? Floyd?"

There was no answer. Floyd lay face down on the pavement. When Adams reached out to touch, him his hand came away sticky with blood.

"Floyd," he said, trying not to panic. He turned him over gently. His face was covered with cuts and bruises that had already started to fade. He was still breathing. Adams let his breath out.

"What happened?" he mused aloud. "Since when can you be taken down by a bunch of henchmen?"

As though in response to his voice Floyd moaned, and his eyes fluttered open.

"Hey," Adams said, taken by surprise. "Are you all right?"

"I'm fine," Floyd lied, sitting up. "Or I will be," he admitted, putting his head in his hands.

"What happened?" Adams repeated. "I heard the henchmen..."

"My head hurts," Floyd complained. "Did I black out?"

"You were unconscious when I got here," Adams confirmed.

"Henchmen..." Floyd started to say, and swore.

"You're sure you're okay?" Adams said anxiously.

"I have an overwhelming urge to go home and sleep," Floyd said. "And my head hurts. But otherwise I'm fine. Thanks for asking."

"Why did the henchmen attack you?" Adams pressed.

"Why do henchmen do anything?" Floyd asked grumpily. "They don't exactly like me, you know."

"But they don't usually try to kill you either."

"They didn't try to kill me," Floyd said. "It was a... a warning. Or a retribution. I don't know. They were acting as a... a collective. It was weird. I usually can handle them."

"But you couldn't this time," Adams pointed out. "What changed?"

"I don't know," Floyd said miserably. "I really don't know." He stared at Adams' hands. "Is that blood?"

"It's yours," Adams said. "They beat you pretty badly."

"I'll live," Floyd said, trying to stand.

"I'm taking you home," Adams decided.

"Why are you always bossing me around?" Floyd said in irritation. But with his first step, he almost fell, and so gratefully flopped one arm over the policeman's shoulder. "Why do I let you boss me around?" he mused as they started off. "I don't have to let you, you know. I'm a grown man, and I can do what I like..."

"Stay awake, Floyd," Adams said warningly.

"I am awake," Floyd argued.

"You're rambling," Adams said. "You always start to ramble when you're about to pass out on me."

"Kate would understand," Floyd mumbled, seemingly not listening to him. "Kate treats me like a grown man."

"Kate treats you like a pet," Adams argued. "And anyhow, if you like her that much, how come you never call?"

"Don't have time..." Floyd said.

"Don't have time for what?"

"For a girlfriend. I've got supervillains to kill and henchmen to fight... why did they pick on me? Why?"

"Just keep talking," Adams said encouragingly. "You'll figure it out."

"Maybe I should," Floyd said.

"Should what?"

"Call."

"That's what I said."

"You treat me like a child," Floyd said.

"You act like a child."

"I'm not a child," he protested sleepily. "I'm not a child. You sound like my sister..."

"I didn't know you had a sister," Adams said with interest.

"Always bossing me around... telling me I'm a no-good loafer..."

"I never tell you that," Adams justified himself. "You're very useful. I even got you a job."

"'One day I'm going to throw you out,' she said," Floyd continued. "'See what it's like to live on your own.'"

Adams shut up and listened in interest.

"'One day you'll have to learn,'" Floyd repeated himself. "And so she did."

"Did what?"

"Threw me out. Sold me to them."

"To who?"

"Them. She was getting married. Her husband didn't want to support me, and I couldn't get any work..."

"It's okay," Adams tried to reassure him. "You have work now."

"I want to go home," Floyd said plaintively.

"We're almost there," Adams said.

"Home..." Floyd whispered, and Adams knew he didn't mean his flat.

"We're almost there," he lied.

COMPUTER FILE 2.5.1
Regeneration

Your first experience with regenerative sleep will be your most unpleasant. That is why it will take place here, in training. In a few moments, you will be shot with a high-power energy rifle that would kill most beings instantly. It will not kill you. However, you may not be able to tell the difference at first. You will become unconscious instantly. You will bleed considerably and your heart may cease to function for several minutes. The nanobots in your bloodstream will ensure that your brain receives enough oxygen to continue to function normally once you wake up.

The nanobots will then begin the healing process. They will inject accelerated healing hormones into your bloodstream to facilitate this as quickly as possible. In this scenario they will work simultaneously to stop the bleeding and to restore normal body functions, such as breathing and a heartbeat.

Once your condition has stabilized, the nanobots will devote themselves entirely to the damage made by the weapon in your chest. We are unsure of how long this process will take. We hope it will be completely in 2-3 days, but it is entirely possible that it will take several weeks. The more extensive damage your body suffers, the longer you will be forced to remain in regenerative sleep. Fatal wounds are always worse than non-fatal injuries, but in some cases may be restored more quickly. Complex systems take longer to heal than simple tasks like replacing blood. Part of this test will be to see how well the regenerative bots perform under emergency situations involving near-death.

The process is exceedingly painful, but you will be unconscious for most of it. However, when you do awake, you will be aware of an intense burning pain on the surface level. This is the last of the regenerative additives burning off. Disorientation is common, since much time will have passed and you won't remember passing out. You may also feel dizzy and lightheaded. It is important to eat as soon as possible after awakening from a regenerative state. You will also need to sleep more than you are accustomed to as your body readjusts to being awake.

A sense of panic will usually be present when you wake up. Try not to give into this urge. It will be difficult, since you won't immediately remember where you are, but it is simply leftover adrenaline in your system resulting from whatever caused you to go into regenerative sleep to begin with.

In extreme cases, some abilities may take longer to return than others. One of the things we hope to observe with this scenario is long-term effects of regenerative sleep. Your responses will be recorded and used in future experiments.

The nanobots are self-replicating, and thus they should last you as long as you need them to. You are intended to stay on earth as long as it takes to complete your task—whether that is ten years or two hundred. The nanobots will not prevent aging, but once triggered, they will restore any abilities you may have lost over the years. The nanobots are programmed with your current brain patterns and abilities so that if you face your first supervillain as an eighty-year-old man and are killed instantly, then you will regenerate as young and healthy as the day you arrived.

This ends the training file on regenerative sleep. The scenario will begin in five, four, three, two, one…

A TIME TO WAIT

Floyd woke up to the sound of someone calling his name. The moment he returned to consciousness, he was assaulted by sensations, thoughts, and reflections in such rapid procession that it made him dizzy. He was hungry. He was thirsty. He was hot and cold at the same time. His head felt like it was stuffed with cotton. Someone was calling his name.

He didn't know where he was. He couldn't remember what had happened. He was dizzy and his body ached, and someone was calling his name.

"Shut up," he muttered, and tried to ignore the voice and go back to sleep. Surely nothing could be so serious that it couldn't wait for him to heal properly.

But the voice didn't shut up. It teased and tugged at him, whispering, singing, silkily worming its way past the confusion and the cotton and urging him back into wakefulness. Floyd obeyed and followed it, puzzled.

"You're not Adams," he said finally, and looked around.

There was nothing to see. It was all dark. He wasn't at home, in bed. He was sitting in the dark... alone...

"Where am I?"

The voice didn't answer. It slithered away and left him alone and freezing cold. He shouldn't be cold. Cold wasn't right. In fact, he was distinctly certain that being cold meant something was wrong. And why in the name of evil couldn't he remember what was going on? Who had been talking to him? Had he been imagining it? Was it a nightmare?

The confusion didn't go away. The darkness didn't go away. Floyd started to get annoyed. He didn't like not knowing what was going on. He didn't like feeling this way either. He wondered what was wrong with him.

He stood up and felt his way around the room. The movement made him sway with dizziness, but he'd done more under worse circumstances. He just wished he could see his surroundings. It was always possible to miss something in the dark, even with a thorough examination.

He wanted to believe he'd missed something, because he hadn't found anything. He slumped back on the metal floor and tried hard not to think about water. There had to be a way in, or he wouldn't be here, which meant that there must be a way out.

Suddenly struck by a sense of deja vu, Floyd tried to reason out what it was that he was missing. He had never been captured before; so why did this situation feel so familiar? His short term memory was missing, again...

And the thought brought him up short. Again? He'd lost his memory once already? That would explain why he couldn't remember—

On the verge of epiphany, he was interrupted by a howling wind that filled his ears and tore him apart bit by bit, scatting the pieces to the farthest reaches of the universe, only to pull him back together with bone-shattering force that landed him firmly inside his own body with his head pounding and his ears ringing. He swore, looked around the darkness in which he could see nothing, and swore again.

There was a voice inside his head laughing at him, genuinely amused at his discomfiture. A point of light appeared in the darkness, coming towards him. At first he thought he was imagining it, but as he stared, it began to grow in size and brightness. He looked away. There was a flash and then the light was gone, mostly. There had to be light somewhere, because he could see the little girl that stood in front of him, but there didn't appear to be any source for the illumination. She didn't glow, and he couldn't see anything else in the room, not even his hand in front of his face, but he could see her.

At least, he thought he could see her. He stared at her, trying to make sure. Her face was serious and she had wide, brown eyes full of knowledge no child should have. Her hair was black and brushed to a shine, and she wore a spotless party dress.

Tired of staring, Floyd blurted out: "Who on earth are you?"

"I am the psychic projection of your captor," the child said, her tone matter-of-fact. "She wished to communicate with you, but has no desire for you to see her true form."

"She?" Floyd said. "I've been captured by a villainess?"

"That is correct. You should have been able to guess it simply by the mere fact of your capture. Women are well known for being more devious than men, and more capable of using their villainous powers to successful ends. They are not as eager for public acclaim as supervillains are, and less likely to fall into the common traps that claim the lives of so many of our kind."

"I don't exactly remember much about my capture," Floyd pointed out.

"We can assist you with that," said the little girl.

"We?" Floyd started, but before he could get the next word out, he was jerked away again. Back into that terrifying night, with the cold rain pelting on his face, mingling with the blood of the many, many villains he had killed already, watching through eyes wide with horror, unable to do anything but watch, it already being too late—

Jerked back to reality, Floyd wrapped his arms around himself, gasping for breath through the ache in his chest and the tightness in his throat he didn't understand. Memories came rushing back, like flood waters bursting through a dam. He was a prisoner. He had been a prisoner for hours, days maybe. He was under the control of villain with incredible powers—

"Villainess," the little girl interrupted.

"Joseph is dead," Floyd said, choking the words out through the lump in his throat, struggling to comprehend what he was saying. "He died fighting for me. I couldn't save him. He died..."

"That is correct," said the child, without emotion. "Sergeant Joseph Adams and twenty other policemen died in the battle to save London. The battle was lost. London is now under the control of the supervillains, and you are our prize."

"Prize." Floyd caught onto the word. "What are you going to do with me?"

"Only whatever strikes the fancy of the Telepath," said the child. "She wishes to see how strong you are; how far your limits will stretch before you break."

"I don't—I don't understand," Floyd said. "I've killed hundreds of supervillains. Don't they want their revenge? Aren't you going to kill me?"

"This is our revenge," said the little girl. "Why kill you when we can force you live on in agony? Your best friend is dead because of you; can you survive the guilt of that? This prison is inescapable. Within these four walls, you can relive that memory until the end of time."

"I'll starve to death eventually," Floyd threatened.

"That is true," the child said. "The nanobots in your bloodstream are powered by the same energy that keeps you alive. If that source of energy is never replenished they will cease to function, as well as your vital systems. We have run the appropriate calculations. You will survive for three weeks, two days, and seventeen hours."

"You've calculated that precisely, eh?" Floyd said, attempting to be sarcastic.

"The Telepath has seen into your mind," said the child. "She understands better than you your physical limitations."

"So you intend to let me die slowly?" Floyd said. "I thought the plan was endless agony."

"The Telepath wishes to play a game with you. If, at the end of the three weeks, two days, and seventeen hours you still have the will to live, you are still your own man, then she will restore your strength and let you live. If she succeeds in breaking you, however, then she will let you die and string your body up in chains upon the very bridge on which you were defeated."

Floyd closed his eyes and shook his head. "Let me get this straight," he said. "If I don't go crazy by the time I die then she's going to let me live until I go crazy?"

"It is not your sanity that the Telapath wishes to claim," said the child. "It is your will."

"That's rather nebulous."

The girl took a step closer, almost human in her sincerity. "Can you refuse to obey her every command, Floyd?" she asked. "Can you look into her eyes and resist the power she has over you? Can you save yourself from begging for mercy at her feet?"

"Stronger people than the Telepath have done worse to me," Floyd said, but it was a hollow boast.

"And when first you came to this planet, you were no more in control of your actions than a blubbering idiot. It will be worse for you than that by the time she is through with you."

The psychic projection began to shrink, and fade away.

"Wait," Floyd said, stalling. "When does this so-called game begin?"

The child faded completely from view. Her voice wafted back to him through the darkness.

"It has already begun."

....

Three weeks. Floyd slumped back against the wall and tried to think it through. Three weeks. This wasn't a game he knew how to play. It wasn't a simple matter of talk-or-die. The Telepath already knew everything about him. Her psychic projection had proven that without even being asked. Any information he was supposed to protect had already been lost. Countless supervillains now knew exactly who he was, where he had come from, and what his weaknesses were. She'd probably pulled all knowledge of the Galactic Alliance from his brain as well, and he'd never even noticed.

No, this villainess was up to something much darker. She wanted to break him, whatever that meant. Floyd stared into the darkness, wishing desperately for something else to stare at, and wondered if it was possible. The people who had trained him had stripped his mind apart and put it back together into the configuration they wanted it to be; the mind of a fighter. Was there anything of his original self even left to be broken? He was sitting alone in the dark, a prisoner of the enemy he'd sworn to defeat, his only friend in the world dead trying to defend him. He didn't have anything left to lose.

He was dying. He was cold and miserable and tired and hungry and Joseph was dead, and he was dying. He had failed in his mission. The world would be overrun by supervillains, and possibly destroyed, unless the Department sent down a replacement. Maybe someone who actually wanted the job. Maybe with better tech. How many years had it been now? Six? Seven? Neural interfaces must have come along quite a bit by now.

Floyd kicked himself. Why was he obsessing over the past? He'd been too busy fighting the Department tooth and nail to argue about what kind of tech they gave him. They wanted him to succeed, so it was doubtful they would have sent him with anything less then the best. Even if all he ended up with was nanobots who were useless against really important stuff like torture, and starvation. He didn't even have a built in torch so he could see his surroundings.

He hadn't thought about it in so long, all the things he no longer had access to. Simple things, like having glowing fingertips or gadgets so small you could embed them in your wrist; activating the display with a mere thought. He'd never had any such bio-upgrades, of course. Couldn't afford them. Anything he did make he usually drank away—

And he laughed bitterly at himself, suddenly realizing what an idiot he'd been then; what an idiot he'd always been. Too wrapped up in himself to notice the world at his feet, and now he was dying, and had nothing at all. Tell most people they're going to die in three weeks and they'll cram every second of the rest of their lives into those few, too-short days. See every sight, greet every friend, say everything they never had a chance to say before. And all he had to look forward to was darkness, and more darkness. The laugh turned sour in his throat, unexpectedly turning into a coughing fit.

He lay exhausted on the cold, metal floor and wondered if the villainess was wrong. If he was this weak already, he'd never make it another twenty-three days.

"We're never wrong," said the child-voice of the telepath's psychic projection. "Our calculations are precise. This weakness you feel now is your body's attempt to convince you to get rest and food. It's amplifying your feelings of exhaustion so that you don't ignore them. Once it realizes that the warning aren't doing any good, you'll feel much better. You might even have hope of escaping us, or exacting retribution. When the true exhaustion comes on, it will be much slower, but lasting. For the last few days you won't be able to move at all. Your nanobots will send you into a coma to preserve as much energy as possible, but you will not be able to escape us there. The only true escape for you will be final and permanent death."

"You have this all figured out," Floyd said in annoyance.

"Your reflections on your past life have been a source of great information to the Telepath," the child continued, ignoring him. "As well as your sense of regret for not doing more while you were free. While such regrets are to be expected from anyone who is as certain of dying as you, surely your efforts towards preserving the world count in some way towards meaningful things you have accomplished in your life. Given the same choice over again, would you not do the exact same thing?"

"Of course I would," Floyd snapped. "I don't have a choice. That's why I got this assignment."

"Of course you have a choice," she argued patiently. "We always have a choice. Between going or staying, good and evil, rebellion or subservience. You can choose now to live or die, and you will choose to live. And you will be given another choice; to die a slave of the Telepath or a servant only to yourself, and which will you choose then?"

"I'll never serve any villain," Floyd said bitterly.

The psychic projection smiled. "We will see," she said simply, and vanished again.

London's Legends: Superhero Vigilante – Fact or Fantasy?
September 2, 2013

Experts tell us that superheroes don't exist, but some locals beg to differ. Marguerite Sanders, age 53 claims to have been rescued from a supervillain by a handsome stranger who appeared out of nowhere.

"One minute I was running for my life and the next this gentleman was helping me up and telling me to stay out of the way," she says, reliving the events of that night. "I didn't know what to do. I was so scared."

Sanders' rescuer then proceeded to take out her pursuers barehanded, saving the victim and taking her home. Sanders was unable to report who was chasing her, or how many there were.

Sanders' story is supported by the reports of other eyewitnesses who claim to have been rescued.

"He said his name was Floyd and that he was a Supervillain hunter." Anne Corrie, age 23, has a star struck look in her eyes as she recounts her tale. "He told me to stand out of the way, and then he just stood there, waiting, as the monster came rushing towards him."

Corrie reports being "scared out of her wits" and "utterly amazed" by her rescuer's daring. But at the last minute the monster screeched to a halt, confused by his prey's boldness and, after shrinking to human form, fell over dead.

To some, these last minute rescues might seem ludicrous, but after hundreds of people witnessed a clone army rushing down Castle Street come suddenly to a halt and vanish, it's hard to disregard the rumours. Over half of the witnesses interviewed reported a man in a black coat rushing out into the army waving a handgun just before the disappearance. The gun was later identified as belonging to Detective Sergeant Joseph Adams but he denies firing the shot. He says he noticed his weapon missing just moments before the incident occurred, and surmised it was stolen by some urchin in the crowd. Sergeant Adams declined to comment further on the incident.

The evidence of a supervillain fighting vigilante seems overwhelming, but does that really contradict the popular scientific notion that there can't be any superheroes? The vigilante, who we believe calls himself "Floyd" has not exhibited any usual signs of superhuman abilities. He's stolen a police officer's gun, consoled an elderly lady chased by gangsters, and frightened an apparition. Is it possible that these are all unrelated incidents attributed to the same growing urban legend?

But is there a dark side to our fairytale hero? Scotland Yard has stepped up their supervillain protocols, even hiring a professional consultant and proposing creating an entire department for handling crimes by supervillains. While this may sound good at the first look, and anonymous source tipped us that there is also a proposal for the implementation of "Emergency Supervillain Measures."

These Emergency Measures would include a curfew, as well as strict limitations on where people would be allowed to travel, and who they could communicate with. By some strange coincidence the author of the proposal is the Yard's newest consultant: Jeffry Lewis Floyd. Is it mere coincidence that Floyd is the name of Anne's rescuer? Or is there something more sinister at play?

What does it mean if the author of this proposal is also masquerading as a vigilante in the street? Who is Jeffry Lewis Floyd? What is the truth behind his proposal? And is the supervillain threat really as great as we've been lead to believe?

A TIME TO TRY

Sergeant Joseph Adams was one of the calmest people Floyd had ever met. He never got upset and rarely raised his voice. So Floyd was more than a little startled when the Sergeant walked, no, charged, into the office one morning, literally howling in rage.

"You double-crossing sneak," he shouted, advancing on Floyd. The smaller man hastened to get out of the way, but he was trapped in the corner and could only retreat so far.

"What are you talking about?" he blustered.

"Are you trying to get fired?" Adams demanded, grabbing him by his shirt-front. "Are you trying to get *me* fired?"

"What?" Floyd said, blinking in confusion. "No! Why would I—no! Joseph—"

The policeman charged ahead without waiting for explanation.

"These kinds of stunts are the reason I never wanted to work with you in the first place," he accused. "You're a risk to the entire department!"

Floyd shoved him away with the strength he usually reserved for fighting the bad guys.

"Stop," he said, furious. "Get out of my face and explain what in the name of sanity you're talking about."

Adams blinked. "You don't know?"

Floyd crossed him arms and glared. "I haven't the slightest idea."

"Haven't you seen the news?"

"No," Floyd said with exaggerated patience. "I have not seen the news. I never watch the news. I am far too busy to deal with the news."

"So you're telling me you don't know that confidential information is currently plastered across the city?"

"No!" Floyd repeated again. "What confidential information? What are you accusing me of?"

Adams shoved a paper into his chest. "Read that," he said.

With another glare at his friend Floyd smoothed the paper out on his desk and read.

As his eyes scanned the words, his expression darkened from mere annoyance to deep concern.

"You see?" Adams said accusingly. "You're telling me you have nothing to do with this?"

"I didn't tell them anything," Floyd said hotly. "What kind of idiot do you take me for?"

"A cocky, over-confident one," Adams retorted.

"True," Floyd admitted, "but I would never do anything like this."

"You've been talking to someone," Adams said. "Where else could they have picked up this information? You and I were the only ones who knew!"

"I showed you the proposal," Floyd countered. "I got beat up by henchmen, and then I went home and stayed in the dark until I came here an hour ago. When would I have talked to someone?"

"That's a pathetic alibi," Adams glowered.

"But it happens to be true," Floyd snapped. "Look at me. You know it's true. I wouldn't do something like this. Why would I do this?"

"Because someone paid you to?"

Floyd flushed angrily. "You pay me well enough," he retorted. "And I'm not a traitor! I may be ruthless, but I'm no traitor. And this—" he slapped the paper, "—this hurts me as much as it does you. I am not responsible for this."

The staring contest endured until Adams let out his breath in a great sigh.

"You're right," he said finally. "I'm sorry. But I had to be sure..."

"And how were you going to make sure?" Floyd asked bitterly. "Lock me up in a cell and torture me until I confessed?"

"By making you angry and looking you in the eye," Adams retorted. "You never lie when you're angry."

"Really?" Floyd said, surprised.

"Really," Adams confirmed.

"I didn't know that."

"Anyway," Adams said, snatching the paper back. "We need to do something with this."

"Yes we do," Floyd agreed.

They stared at each other again.

"Well don't look at me!" Floyd exclaimed. "I'm not going to pull something out of my hat and fix it all."

"Why not?" Adams asked, a teasing edge coming into his voice. "It's what you usually do."

"Well, this isn't usual," Floyd said. "Henchmen don't usually gang up in alleyways to confront their fears in broad daylight. The newspapers don't usually notice I exist. Something has changed."

"How so?"

"I don't know," he said, frustrated. "It's just— a feeling. Not a good one."

"So you're going to sit here and do nothing because you have a bad feeling?" Adams said dubiously.

"What else can I do?" Floyd asked.

"Find them," Adams said, gesturing. "Stop the bad guys. Do what you always do."

"What bad guys?" Floyd countered. "We're talking about the media here. They can't be stopped. Or are you telling me to go kill every reporter who mentions my name?"

Adams sighed and paused a moment to collect his thoughts. "No, I'm not telling you to kill anybody," he said patiently. "But you can't just ignore the problem either."

"Why not?" Floyd asked, crumpling up the paper and throwing it in the wastebasket.

"Because it won't just go away if you pretend it doesn't exist," Adams said.

"So?" Floyd stood up, and grabbed his coat. "If I pretend it doesn't exist at least it won't bother me for a few days."

"Until the next time someone tries to kill you?"

Floyd grinned viciously. "Exactly."

"That's a terrible plan!"

"Who said it was a plan at all? I just don't want to deal with it. So lay off already."

Adams grabbed Floyd's arm as he tried to walk out the door.

"You are not leaving this room until I get a straight answer out of you," he growled.

Floyd yanked free, the expression on his face unreadable.

"I'm just tired, okay?" he snapped. "Digging into this... it's going to turn up something ugly and I don't want to deal with it. I'm tired of fighting the monsters. I'm tired of getting my bones broken every week and waking up on fire from regeneration. So the media is on my back now as well. Fine. I don't care. I'm going to go home and get some proper sleep."

"And I repeat," Adams said. "That's a terrible plan."

"Then you come up with the plans for once," Floyd said. "And when you do, come let me know."

Adams opened his mouth, and shut it again when no retort came out. Floyd straightened his coat and left the room.

COMPUTER FILE 5.7.3
Pain

It is extremely unlikely that you will ever be captured. However, on occasion, you may need to infiltrate a supervillain's lair by pretending to be an ordinary human. In these circumstances, you may be subjected to certain unpleasant treatment, such as torture or experimentation.

Under no circumstances are you to ever allow yourself to be tested or examined. Never let anyone get a sample of your blood. You should always exercise the greatest care to avoid bleeding where traces might be picked up by supervillains or their henchmen. The alterations we have made to your physical and chemical make-up are top-secret and could have disastrous consequences were they ever discovered by humans, super or otherwise.

The easiest way to cope with pain is, of course, to distance yourself from it. You must learn to separate your mind from your body, so that the punishment of the latter does not affect the proper functions of the former. There are many methods of conditioning yourself to endure pain, some of which we will be covering in later sessions. Along with the extremely slim chance of enduring torture there is the much more common injuries associated with battling supervillains, not to mention regeneration.

A TIME TO WEEP

Floyd's world had been reduced to two things. Darkness and... well, really there was just the darkness. Occasionally it was intimidating, sometimes it was stifling, but mostly it was exceedingly boring. The pounding headache he had as a result of dehydration only intensified the boredom. Having nothing to do besides measure his heartbeat as it pounded against his temples only made the experience worse.

"Hello?" he called out experimentally into the darkness. "Do you want to... gloat or something? I'm available for gloating at, if you're interested."

His voice reverberated off the metal walls and faded away. Floyd twitched with impatience.

"This isn't how you play the game," he scolded. "There's supposed to be fire and questions and other nasty stuff."

Again, no answer.

"Really?" he said, ignoring the fact that talking made his headache worse, and his throat itch. "What kind of a villain are you that the prospect of blood and pain doesn't entice you to come out and play? Even that annoying little girl would be better than—"

He stopped to cough, and the psychic projection appeared instantly, her childish face frowning in a pout.

"I'm not an annoying little girl," she said pointedly. "I am the psychic projection of your captor."

"Yeah, I got that the first time," Floyd said. "But you are too annoying. And what's the point of being a child anyway? Is there some deep-seated psychological reason for that?"

"I did not come here to amuse you by answering your questions," said the psychic projection.

Floyd smiled wanly. "Sure you did," he answered with confidence. "You came to gloat. I knew you couldn't resist."

"Your distaste for children is well-known to us," said the child. "The sense that you are being controlled by a child will add to your already overwhelming sense of failure."

"Failure?" Floyd scoffed. "I don't feel a sense of failure. I haven't failed anything yet."

"Your attempts at bravado are pointless when in the presence of one who can read your thoughts. It would be better for you to yield now."

"Don't start on that worship thing again," Floyd said threateningly.

"Perhaps you would prefer..." the child paused to recall his exact words. "Blood and pain?"

Floyd shrugged. "Sure, why not?" he said carelessly. "It would break the monotony."

"Are you not afraid it would break you?"

"I trained for this," he said, a hint of pride coming into his voice. "I'm good at screaming. And the not-answering," he added as an afterthought.

"There is no point in questioning you," said the child haughtily. "We already know the answers."

"You could pretend..." Floyd said hopefully.

"Your desire to be tortured for information is a feeble attempt to make you feel that your death will have some kind of meaning," said the psychic projection. "If you die bravely protecting secrets you are entrusted with, then you can regard yourself as a hero to the people you are sworn to protect."

"Yeah, sure," Floyd grumbled. "Go ahead and make me feel useless all over again. What am I doing here, then, if not to be tortured for information? That's what's *supposed* to happen. That's what they *told* me would happen. Either torture me or kill me, that's my motto."

"You already know what purpose the Telepath wishes to accomplish by holding you here."

"And yet, when I yelled loudly enough, she answered," Floyd pointed out. "See, the Telepath has an ego too."

"Do not underestimate the Telepath," said the child warningly. "She has complete control of your mind, including the nerve centers and pain receptors. Her thoughts can cause unbearable agony that no physical torture could obtain."

"That's what I'm talking about," Floyd said. "Pain and agony. Stuff I can understand, rather than this meaningless psychological mumbo."

"You speak foolishness born from lack of understanding. Do not tempt her."

"Don't tempt her?" Floyd said in disbelief. "Do you know who you're talking to? I don't have anything better to do, and I don't have anything to lose. Anything is better than this monotony, even if it means searing, blinding, mind-numbing—"

He broke off suddenly, as the child pointed a single finger in his direction. She lowered her hand and, after a long moment, he dared to breathe again.

"Okay..." he said slowly. "Maybe not."

He lowered his face into his hands, suddenly devoid of any desire to continue the conversation.

"Is that it?" the psychic projection taunted, throwing his own words back at him. "Aren't you going to beg for more?"

Floyd didn't answer.

"All that talk, and five seconds is enough to silence you," the psychic projection said. "What's the matter, didn't you enjoy your taste of pain and agony? Perhaps you might enjoy a more inventive form of torture."

Floyd looked up, struggling not to say what he was thinking. The child said it for him.

"You're going to die here," she said simply. "One way or another. You can die in mindless agony or you can die in bliss. The question is, which will you choose? Will you surrender to her?"

Floyd answered, with strength he didn't know he had: "Never."

The child smiled, an expression chillingly wrong on her innocent face.

"Then let's see how well you've been trained."

....

Children have a short attention span. The Telepath wasn't a child, but her psychic projection was, whether she would admit it or not. Soon enough she got bored, and wandered off, and Floyd was left with the darkness.

Which was a relief, at first, and then became less of a blessing and more of a curse as time dragged along like a child at an unwilling task. Floyd was left alone with his memories and his thoughts. His thoughts were less painful then the memories, but they were nothing but lingering echoes of the Telepath's threats, as voiced by her child-herald.

You're going to die here.

The truth hit like a fall down an airshaft, but he didn't know what to do with the fact. He didn't know whether to be scared or relieved or disbelieving. He'd died so many times already; what would it be like to never wake up? The thought was frightening and enticing at the same time. But mostly frightening.

The darkness was cold now, and malevolent. Floyd shivered and wrapped his arms around himself, but the cold came from inside. He didn't want to die.

He didn't have a choice.

You're going to die here.

The darkness was overwhelming, blinding, stifling, and he was afraid.

Floyd closed his eyes and counted slowly, willing himself into acceptance.

"The Telepath is disappointed in you."

The psychic projection startled him, and he stared, scrambling for an answer.

"Disappointed?" he stammered. "I—I don't even know how to begin to explain everything that's wrong with that statement."

He was torn between hope and relief, and fear and shame. Finally having something to direct his frustration at, he tried to get his emotions under control, to not let her see what he was going through, to be as sharp with her as he had ever been.

The child frowned. "You don't learn, do you?" she taunted. "We know exactly how you feel. You can't hide anything from us. You are content to accept your fate. The Telepath expected more."

"More, or less?" Floyd asked. "Because, with a villain, you can never tell what they really mean."

"You have made no attempt to regain your freedom, or escape the torment she has inflicted upon you."

"I was asking for it, wasn't I?" Floyd snapped back. "Besides, I thought the game was that winning meant surviving the torment, not avoiding it."

"You expect a villainess to keep her word?"

"I thought it was worth a shot."

"But winning the game will result in your death," the child said, puzzled.

Floyd smiled smugly. "Maybe, maybe not."

"You're a pathetic fool," she snipped, taking a step back.

"So I've been told," Floyd countered.

"There will be consequences for your attitude," she threatened.

He wasn't intimidated. "That's hilarious, coming from you."

"You should show more respect," she warned.

"To a supervillain who doesn't even dare show me her own face?" Floyd said incredulously. "What has she got to be so ashamed of? Or is that her weakness? Maybe she doesn't have a face. Maybe she doesn't actually exist."

The psychic projection faded out of existence while he was still talking. Floyd stared at the darkness where the child had been, overwhelmed by the sudden freezing cold.

"Wait," he called after her. "I'm sorry. What did I say?"

There was no answer. "I didn't mean—" he tripped over his words, not sure why he was apologizing to a villain, not sure why he cared so much for the company of a torturer.

"Please, come back," he said softly. "Look, I'm doing what you asked. I'm begging. Just—"

He knew it was hopeless. He took a deep breath, swallowed, and said it anyway.

"Don't leave me alone."

SUPERVILLAINS OF LONDON
COME OUT OF HIDING
September 9, 2013

The world was stunned today when the so-called supervillains living in London came out of hiding to announce that they were "tired of being hunted like animals."

In a press conference earlier today, supervillain mastermind Rex King Cobra said that supervillains mean no harm to British citizens. Cobra approached the press at great personal risk to ask for an interview. He says he speaks on behalf of the Supervillains of London. Their hope is to bring about an end to the so-called supervillain war.

"Can anyone prove that we've assaulted an innocent person?" Spokesperson Cobra said. "The only time casualties have occurred have been when someone attempted to interfere with us. We reacted in self-defense."

Cobra went on to say that the supervillains feel threatened. He said that the discrimination against them is unethical and unworthy of the British people.

"We're people, too." was Cobra's final statement. "All we ask is the right to live our lives like any other British citizen—peaceably and unafraid for our lives."

What does this statement mean? All over the world, the superhumans have been assumed to be malevolent, but is it possible that we have been wrong all the while? That, in fact, the so-called supervillains are simply our misunderstood altered neighbours?

A TIME TO PRAY

The door to Floyd's apartment creaked open halfway and then refused to budge any further. Sergeant Adams sighed, and squeezed through the opening.

"Floyd?" he called into the dark interior.

"Go away and leave me alone," the alien retorted instantly.

Adams located him by the glow of his laptop screen. His face was contorted into a scowl as he read.

"I take it you've seen the news?" Adams asked.

"Oh, I've seen the news," Floyd said caustically.

"Do you mind if I turn on the light?" Adams said patiently.

Floyd waved one hand. "Be my guest."

Adams located the switch and turned it on. Nothing happened. He sighed and perched on the edge of the sofa.

"It isn't healthy, you know," he lectured. "Living like this."

"You know what isn't healthy?" Floyd retorted. "Getting killed twice a week."

Adams had no answer to that. "Are you angry with me?" he asked, puzzled.

"No," Floyd snapped. "Why would I be angry with you? All you did was accuse me of selling out to a bunch of reporters. For money."

He slammed the laptop closed and turned his full attention to Adams. "Do I *look* like a person who does things for money? What are you even doing here?"

"I came to check on you," Adams said.

"Who asked?"

"It's what I do," Adams retorted. "Someone's trying to kill my best consultant. I'd rather that they didn't succeed."

"I can take care of myself," Floyd said.

"Sure," Adams agreed.

Floyd paused. "Are you mocking me?"

"I learned from the best," Adams retorted. "Are you coming back to the Yard with me?"

"Oh, sure," Floyd grumbled, stuffing his laptop into a bag. "Fine. Whatever."

"You're in a real good mood, aren't you," Adams said sarcastically.

Floyd didn't answer. He followed Adams out of the flat, yanked the door shut behind him, and they traipsed down the dingy stairs into the daylight of the street below.

"Tell me about henchmen," Adams instructed.

Floyd shrugged. "What do you want to know?"

"All the things you never told me because you assumed I knew," Adams said.

"Okay, fine," Floyd said, still in a bad mood. "There are three classes of supervillains, right? Top level is the masterminds. Middle level, supervillains. Lowest level, henchmen. Henchmen are supervillains who have really useless superpowers, or who are really stupid. Masterminds can control other villains using drugs, threats, mind control, bribery, whatever. Supervillains control henchmen by the same means, only without having to be super-intelligent. Even ordinary people can control henchmen if they put some effort into it."

"Ordinary people... like you?" Adams asked.

Floyd flushed. "They're not a threat, okay?" he said defensively. "They're just really stupid and sometimes helpful. They have no sense of loyalty, and it's pretty easy to get information out of them."

"They seemed to be a threat the other day," Adams observed.

"That's not normal," Floyd retorted. "I told you that already. I don't know how and I don't know why, but they were acting intelligent, and it's not normal. Because the first rule of henchmen is that they're stupid."

"Never underestimate your enemy," Adams replied swiftly.

"I didn't underestimate them!" Floyd shouted in frustration. "They—they changed."

"Changed how?" Adams persevered.

"I don't know," Floyd said. "Collectively they were acting smart. Intelligent. Like a—"

"Hive," Adams said instantly.

"What?" Floyd asked.

"There are certain insects that, individually, are practically brainless, but operating together their collective intelligence is fairly impressive," Adams explained. "The phenomena has lead to the science fiction theory of a hive mind."

Floyd stared. "That's unsettlingly accurate," he said.

"That's why you should talk to me more," Adams said placidly.

"Fine." Floyd flung up both hands in surrender. "I'm sorry. I was acting like an idiot."

"That's better," Adams said, smiling. "So now let's talk about supervillains."

"Do you need a primer on them too?" Floyd taunted.

"I want to talk about the ones who claim they're not evil," Adams corrected.

"That's absolute hogwash," Floyd scoffed. "And you know it."

"I don't know," Adams said doubtfully. "The press seems to be taking them seriously enough."

"Then the press are morons," Floyd said.

"Granted," Adams said. "But people listen to them."

"And people are morons," Floyd said quickly. "We established this already. It doesn't make it any less ridiculous."

"Being ridiculous doesn't make it any less real," Adams countered. "Don't underestimate the enemy."

"I'm not underestimating them!" Floyd shouted. "Why do you keep saying that?"

"Things are changing," Adams said patiently. "You keep telling me that. Nothing is the way you expect it to be, and if you don't change with it you're going to end up dead."

"That's a pathetic threat to make to someone who can't die," Floyd said, rolling his eyes.

"Be careful," Adams warned.

"Fine," Floyd said shortly.

"So," Adams prompted. "What can you tell me about these supervillains? What are they up to? What's their motivation?"

Floyd shrugged. "I have no idea."

"That's really helpful."

"I have to gather some more information," Floyd said.

"And how are you going to do that?"

"I'm going to go threaten a henchman. Are you coming along?"

Adams grinned. "How can I possibly pass up an invitation like that?" he asked.

....

"Kelly!" Floyd shouted jovially, as though greeting an old friend. The supervillain looked up in surprise at having his haven disturbed. The basement he lived in was filled with monitors and computer equipment of all kinds.

"Watch your feet," he snapped at Adams, who was suddenly struck by a sensation of familiarity.

"Wait, I know this guy," he said to Floyd. "You're that ninja guy, right? The Black Shadow?"

The villain sighed in exaggerated patience. "Great, you've heard of me," he said sarcastically. "No! I am not the Black Shadow." He diverted his attention to Floyd. "I thought you were going to fix that?"

"I did," Floyd said calmly. "He just doesn't keep up."

"Didn't we run into him back in May?" Adams asked. "Why is he still around? I thought supervillains had a pretty short lifespan."

"They do," Floyd said enigmatically. "But Kelly here isn't a supervillain. Are you, Kelly?"

"What?" Adams said, startled.

"What?" Kelly said at the same time, indignant.

"Just answer the question," Floyd said.

"I'm not going to answer the question," Kelly said, bristling. "It's an insulting question. Of course I'm a supervillain."

"Sure you are," Floyd said patronizingly. "What's your superpower?"

Kelly puffed out his chest. "Technical Genius," he announced proudly.

"Not a superpower," Floyd retorted. "People are born every day with that. Ordinary people."

"I don't understand," Adams said, rubbing his forehead. "Why would he say he's a supervillain if he's not?"

Floyd laughed. "You're asking me why a nerdy teenager lied?" he asked.

"I'm a geek, not a nerd," Kelly protested indignantly.

"Whatever," Floyd said dismissively.

"I'm asking," Adams said firmly. "Why did you claim to be a supervillain if you're not really?"

Kelly shrugged. "I thought maybe people would take me seriously," he said.

"Guess what?" Floyd said. "It paid off. We're taking you seriously."

"You're mocking me," Kelly said in an injured tone.

"Yes," Floyd admitted, "but we're also taking you seriously. You keep up with the supervillains' activities, right?"

"Yeah, so?"

"So you're going to get some information for me," Floyd said, grinning.

Kelly stared. "I am?"

"You are," Floyd said confidently.

"Why would I help you?" Kelly asked.

"I need your computers," Floyd explained. "And if you don't help, then Sergeant Adams is going to arrest you."

"I am?" Adams said, startled.

"You have your own computers back at Scotland Yard!" Kelly protested.

Floyd was taken aback. "How do you know where I work?" he demanded.

Kelly shrugged. "Everyone knows it," he said. "It's all over the networks."

"I told you so," Adams said smugly.

"Guess what?" Floyd said, recovering control of the situation.

"What?"

"Now you do, too," Floyd said. "Get to work."

"I do what?" Kelly asked, confused.

"Work for Scotland Yard," Floyd explained. "Get busy. I want to know stuff."

"I'm not working for you!" Kelly protested. "I can't! Do you know what they'd do to me if they found out? They'd kill me!"

"Do you know what I'll do to you if you don't?" Floyd retorted.

They locked gazes. "That's right," Floyd continued. "I work for the police now."

Kelly looked away first. "What do you want to know?" he asked sullenly.

"What are the henchmen up to?" Floyd asked quickly. "Why are the supervillains pretending to be good-hearted? Why are the—"

"One question at a time!" Kelly interrupted. "You mean you don't know?"

"Don't know what?" Floyd asked, blinking.

"About the henchman network?" Kelly asked, stating the obvious.

"What henchman network?" Floyd asked.

Inexplicably, Kelly began to laugh. "You don't know!" he exclaimed. "You, of all people!"

"Know what?" Floyd asked in irritation. "Get a grip, and tell me what it is that I don't know! What henchman network?"

"I practically told you," Kelly snickered. "The last time you barged in here uninvited."

"Told me what?" Floyd snapped. "Tell me, now. Or I'll wring your little neck."

"Calm down," Kelly said, taking a step backwards. "The henchmen have developed a communication network. It's city-wide. They're talking about going regional; even global."

"Talking?" Floyd repeated. "They have the intelligence of a chimpanzee."

"Until recently," Kelly corrected. "Collectively, they're quite intelligent. It's like a hive mind."

"I told you so," Adams repeated.

"You know, it's really annoying when you do that," Floyd snapped in irritation.

"It's quite fascinating," Kelly continued. "They have their own dialect, and there are stations set up in hidden locations. They have chatrooms and everything."

"But why?" Floyd said. "What's the point?"

"They use it to exchange information to each other's mutual advantage," Kelly explained. "They obtain information to flatter and appease their superiors rapidly and with fair accuracy. They also use it to commiserate over their state in life, and exchange tips on how to avoid getting murdered in a fit of rage."

"That must be fascinating to study," Floyd said sarcastically. "What have they been up to recently?"

"Well, the last few weeks they've been talking about you a lot, actually," Kelly said, and snickered again. "There was a lot of talk about an ambush or maybe a warning of some kind? It's a bit garbled. But the short version is that they've decided you're a threat."

"They can't be that intelligent if it took them this long to figure that out," Adams observed.

"Shut up," Floyd snapped.

"There's more to it than that, though," Kelly continued. "The supervillains coming out of hiding? They organized that, too. They've individually manipulated their masters into doing exactly what they want."

"That's—scary," Floyd admitted.

"Yeah, it is," Kelly agreed. "Now you see why I think that you guys should get out of here? Go into hiding or something. Wait for it to blow up in their faces. Supervillain alliances never last long; you said that yourself."

"Wait," Adams said, speaking into the silence left by Floyd's lack of response. "What is it that they want? The supervillains, I mean. Why are they coming out like this?"

"Oh, that's simple," Kelly said. "They want Floyd."

COMPUTER FILE 7.3.8
Killing

Your background indicates that you have had no prior experience in killing. Your primary task as Defender of Earth will be to kill supervillains. You may find this objectionable at first, but the purpose of this course is to desensitize you to such things as blood, gore, and to teach you how to deal with things such as pleas for mercy.

Under no circumstances should you ever leave a villain alive. They are adept liars and even if they should happen to tell the truth about that bomb, their girlfriend, or your own conscience, whatever it is they're threatening is less of a disaster than what would result if you fail to take their lives.

In some societies, killing without mercy is frowned upon. You come from one such society. Most Earth cultures will consider killing the sole department of the state, and your actions may be considered the illegal work of a vigilante. You must resist any pressure to conform to socially acceptable guidelines regarding the taking of life.

The following scenarios will guide you through helping you learn to make the right decision when you are faced with a choice in killing a supervillain or some less lethal means of dealing with him. As always, each scenario will repeat until you have mastered the lesson it contains. First scenario beginning in five, four, three, two, one…

Dreams and Shadows

A TIME TO SLEEP

Floyd was telling himself a story. It went something like this.

Once upon a time, there was a self-centered, juvenile young man living on the most beautiful planet in space. He had lost his parents when he was very young, and his sister had lived with the responsibility of raising him. In exchange for this dutiful behavior on her part, the young man repaid her by being nothing but trouble from dawn until evenfall.

But then he had been given a chance to redeem himself. He had been chosen out of millions to receive elite training and become the defender of another world. This world was not as beautiful as his own, but it needed him. However, instead of being grateful for this chance to make something of himself, he complained about his fate and blamed the people who had sent him for their unjustness. And in the end—

Floyd shook his head, as if the gesture could somehow dislodge the thought.

"I did the best I could," he whispered, and he didn't know if he was lying or not.

His reverie was disturbed by the sudden appearance of light in his cell. Real, physical light that burned after being in the dark for so long. He yelped and closed his eyes, turning away from the glare. Rough hands reached out and pulled him to his feet, stuffing a bag over his head, and dragging him across the stone with no concern for whether or not he'd managed to get his feet under him first.

He quickly lost all sense of direction, only barely managing to notice the flight of stairs they went up before he was unceremoniously deposited on a floor that was hard, cold, and remarkably smooth. The bag was snatched off of his head and he blinked at a limited view of a well-decorated room full of henchmen and supervillains.

Soles clicked on the marble floor, eventually bringing a pair of polished black leather boots into his field of vision.

"Is he dead?" asked the familiar, cultured voice that belonged to the owner of the boots.

"Not yet," one of the henchmen replied. "I don't think."

Floyd ignored them all.

"He looks dead," the villain said. "Fetch some water."

Floyd gasped as a bucket of cold water was dumped over him. He was surprised to discover that he could sit up without pain, although moving made him dizzy, and he realised exactly how thirsty he was.

"Well, look who's decided to rejoin the land of the living," the villain said, and all the others

70

laughed. "Get the survivor something to drink, I want to hear what he has to tell us about the afterlife."

Floyd accepted the proffered drink gratefully, and the room stopped tilting.

"Well?" the villain asked. "How do you feel?"

Floyd grinned. "Like taking out a couple of you," he taunted, and was immensely gratified to see the henchmen nearest to him take an instinctive step backwards.

"So," said the villain, in a pompous tone. "We meet again."

The voice was familiar. Familiar enough that Floyd decided he was not going to appear to be inferior to him.

"Indeed we do," he said, mimicking his tone and trying to smile. "I have longed for this momentous occasion."

The villain paused for a moment, but quickly recovered himself. "You're not nearly as fearsome as you were the last time we met," he said. "Up close, without the powerful weapons and back-up, you're quite pitiful, really."

The voice teased at his memory, but he couldn't place it. He cocked his head to see the villain more clearly.

"Have we met?" he said finally.

The villain paused again. "You don't remember?" he queried.

"Short term memory loss," Floyd explained. "It happens after severe injuries. Apparently it becomes permanent when the severe injuries are followed by prolonged starvation."

"That's good to know," said the villain smugly. "I'll remember it the next time I have to deal with an enhanced supervillain killer from another planet."

Floyd smiled again. "Oh, I doubt you'll be around long enough to meet someone else like me," he taunted.

"With the knowledge we have gained from you, no one will be able to stop us," the villain bragged.

"Excuse me," Floyd said sharply. "Don't you mean the knowledge *she* has gained from me? I don't think she's the sort of person who would like being deprived of the full credit for my capture. And you really haven't been around much."

"She couldn't have done it without us," the villain insisted. "Without *me*."

"Oh, all right," Floyd said. "If that makes you feel better then keep telling yourself that."

"Tell me what you mean," said the villain, confused.

"Nothing," Floyd said dismissively. "Forget I said anything."

"Tell me what you meant, scum," the villain threatened, "Or I will—"

Floyd laughed. "I wouldn't, if I were you," he said. "I'm pretty sure she wants me kept in good condition."

The villain struggled to contain his rage. "You will die a long and agonizing death," he said.

"Been there, done that," Floyd feigned boredom. "Have anything original to say?"

The villain hissed in displeasure and walked a few steps away.

"What am I doing here anyway?" Floyd asked. "I spend weeks locked in a dungeon, alone, talking to voices in my head, and then suddenly you guys show up. Not that I'm not glad to see you, or anything," he clarified. "Because I am. I really am."

The villain smiled superciliously.

"She has that effect on all of us, if it's any consolation," he sneered. "You needn't be ashamed of your *weakness*. You've defeated many, many supervillains. You would probably have defeated us as well if not for the Telepath."

"You wanted to defeat me that badly," Floyd said hollowly.

"Of course," the villain said with a smile. "You're the only thing that stands between us and ruling the galaxy."

"Actually," Floyd snapped, "There's an entire galaxy out there that will stop you if I fail."

The villain gestured condescendingly. "They're nothing."

"They created me," Floyd pointed out.

"We'll deal with them," the villain said confidently. "We just have to deal with this planet first, and thanks to her, victory is within our grasp."

"Have we met before?" Floyd demanded, the villain's name still evading him. "I still can't remember your name."

"Temporary memory block," the villain explained. "She wants you to stay that way."

"Why?"

"To drive you insane, of course."

Floyd fought back despair. Here in this room, he felt real. These were people he could understand and compared to the dark and the Telepath, they were almost friends.

"Will you do me a favour?" he asked abruptly.

The villain laughed. The room laughed with him. Floyd didn't care, and waited for them to ask the inevitable question...

"What favour?" the villain asked. "What could you possibly expect us to do for you?"

"Will you kill me?" Floyd asked.

The abruptness of his request silenced the room.

"I don't care what you have to do," he said desperately. "Cut off my head, burn my body, I don't care. I just want to die."

"That's a very tempting offer," the villain said slowly. "But I'm afraid we'll have to decline. As you said, she wants you preserved as much as possible."

"Then why am I here?" Floyd said desperately. He glanced around the room. "There's got to be at least two hundred of you here. And why, to gloat? You can't be expected to keep them all under control. If there were to be an accident—"

The other villains and henchmen laughed, but Floyd didn't know if they were laughing at him or at the prospect for killing him.

"Enough!" the villain snapped, and to Floyd's surprise the others obeyed. Silence fell.

The villain leaned down to peer into Floyd's eyes, and seemed surprised at what he saw there.

"She's really got to you," he said softly.

"Please," Floyd whispered. "Please don't send me back to that cell alive."

The villain smiled. "No," he said simply, and walked away.

"She's controlling you!" Floyd shouted at his back. "You think you're immune because you're a supervillain too? Villains never work together."

The retreating figure froze.

"You know I'm telling the truth," Floyd continued recklessly. "Help me, and I'll help you. I can take her out for you, and you can be free again. We can go back to how things were."

The villain smiled. "Why would we want that?" he asked. "She has given us everything we want."

"For now, maybe," Floyd floundered. "What happens when she has everything she wants? What further use will she have for you then?"

"A pity you won't be around to see," the villain said coldly. "We will rule this world together."

"Keep lying to yourself," Floyd said. "If it makes you feel better."

The villain frowned. "You said that before," he observed. "You never explained what you meant."

"You know what I mean," Floyd said.

"Tell me," the villain hissed.

Floyd beckoned him to come closer. The villain bent down, listening.

"When the Telepath is done with me," Floyd whispered, "who do you think will be her next plaything?"

The villain's face darkened in rage. He raised his hand to strike, but someone from the crowd stopped him.

"Don't give him what he wants," said the new voice. "It is better to trust her."

Slowly, the leader lowered his hand. He took a deep breath and smiled down at Floyd.

"Take him away," he ordered.

He gestured and two henchmen came forward, grinning.

"No," Floyd said, panicking, trying to stand and get away. "No, you can't send me back there. Please..."

The darkness surrounded him, already becoming a reality. They grabbed his arms and hauled him to his feet. "You can't send me back to her!" Floyd shouted. He looked around for sympathy, but these were supervillains, and they had no mercy.

"Look who's afraid," the villain sneered. "There's a sight worth waiting for. The brave supervillain killer pleading just to die."

"Name your price," Floyd said. "I'll give you anything you want."

"You have nothing to give," said the nameless leader carelessly.

The room they were in was rich, and well decorated. Long windows overlooked a courtyard. Weapons were displayed between them. With the desperate strength of a madman, Floyd broke away from the villains holding him and leapt for one of the swords on the wall. He pulled it down, and turned to defend himself, but there were too many. Even at his best he could never defeat them all. He struggled to reach a window, but they pressed around him, and he went down under the blows.

Every villain in the room wanted a chance at him, unable to resist once the melee had begun. They crowded around him laughing, crowing, kicking, tearing, breaking bones, until finally the leader made himself heard, and they backed off sullenly, leaving Floyd hovering on the edge of oblivion.

The villain approached, and stared down at him in derision. He picked up the sword Floyd had dropped, and swung it around, clearly unable to resist. Floyd closed his eyes and looked away, as he raised it above his head and drove it into his body.

His sneer was the last thing Floyd saw as his world faded to black.

ALTERED HUMANS SAY THEY COME IN PEACE. OFFICIALS DISAGREE.

September 16, 2013

The supervillain situation continues, with new superhumans emerging all over the city and demanding equal treatment as British citizens. But not all are as welcoming to this new turn of events as the so-called villains would hope. Unnamed officials have expressed some alarm at the number of supervillains in the city. Experts tell us that these numbers mean that almost 10% of the world's population could be altered humans.

The Metropolitan Police Force especially continues to call for strict measures in dealing with what they've determined is a threat to national security. They say that the supervillains' claim for peace is nothing but alligator tears, and that they are not to be trusted. They point out that such incidents as the horrendous fires experienced last spring were the work of malicious altered humans.

However, the proposal for Emergency Supervillain Measures, including a proposed curfew, has upset many people. Supervillain consultant for Scotland Yard, Jeffry Lewis Floyd, maintains that "the supervillain threat is not and never has been taken seriously by the British people." Questions have been raised about Floyd's background and expertise. Previously accused of working as a vigilante, nothing concrete can be turned up on who he is, or where he came from. The Chief Inspector is not available to comment on his decision to hire Floyd as a consultant.

Rex King Cobra insists that Floyd is a merciless supervillain hunter and described him as: "A racist vigilante with a god-complex" and a threat to everybody, not just the superhumans. The infamous Floyd has been himself mysteriously absent. Reporters attempting to interview him have found him conveniently out of office, and he appears to have no phone number at which he can be reached. These and similar oddities have led some to wonder if, perhaps, reports of Floyd's existence have been greatly exaggerated.

A TIME TO SAY

"Of course they want me," Floyd was saying as they walked back to Scotland Yard. "The supervillains always want me. What else is new?"

"Working together is new," Adams said pragmatically. "The henchmen being in control as a hive mind is new."

"So how does that change anything?" Floyd asked.

"It means they might actually succeed," Adams retorted. "You need to take this seriously, Floyd. Do you even have any kind of plan?"

Floyd shrugged and got out of answering by running up the steps of Scotland Yard to get the door.

Waiting on the other side was the Chief Inspector.

"Excuse me, sir," Floyd stammered, glancing around for Adams. "I didn't see—"

"Where have you been?" demanded the chief. "I've been wanting to talk to you."

"Working, actually," Floyd said. "I've been following a lead on the Rex King Cobra; what his agenda is, who he's working for—"

"Never mind that," the chief interrupted. "You're off the case."

Floyd gaped. "What do you mean, off the case?" he asked. "You can't stop me from tracking down supervillains; it's what I do!"

"Not this one," the chief inspector said, shaking his head. "It's too dangerous."

"I know the risks," Floyd said stubbornly. "And, frankly, there's no one better qualified then I am."

"Have you seen the news today?" the chief demanded.

"No," Floyd said shortly. "I'm still dealing with the news from yesterday."

"So you don't know what's going on then," the chief said grimly. "Come see this. Sergeant!"

Adams jumped to attention and followed them.

"I have no idea what's going on," Floyd grumbled as he followed obediently. "The entire world is going insane, human and 'superhuman' alike."

The policemen ignored him.

"Read this," the inspector ordered, handing Floyd a newspaper.

Floyd read, his forehead crinkling in distaste.

"Well, he's not lying," he said finally. "Except about the god complex bit. I really do kill them without discrimination, and I really am a threat to their survival. And I thought that's what I was supposed to be."

"There are starting to be people who disagree," the chief said. "There's a new movement of sympathizers with the superhumans. Their slogan is 'Supervillains are people, too.'"

"Superhumans?" Floyd scoffed. "You sound just like them."

"Emotions are very high right now," the chief warned. "We could end up with a lynch mob screaming for your head."

"I could handle them," Floyd said confidently.

"Not if they were human," Adams warned.

"We could get an order to detain you," the chief warned.

"You won't let that happen," Floyd said confidently.

"I'm trying," the chief inspector said patiently. "So here's the plan. You need to disappear for a while."

"That's the plan?" Floyd said dubiously. "You want me to just... run and hide?"

"Until all this dies down," the chief said, "That's the safest thing for you and for us."

"I don't care about being safe," Floyd said bitterly. "I've never run from a fight in my life."

"This isn't a fight you can win, Floyd," Adams said gently.

"You're siding with him?" Floyd exclaimed, whirling on his friend.

"I agree with him," Adams said. "Don't play into their hands."

"They're not hurting anyone for now," the chief added. "Let's give it some time and let it play out. See what their next move is."

"Time is exactly what you never give an evil mastermind who's trying to rule the world," Floyd snapped. "We need to go after them now."

"Against public opinion?" Adams asked.

"Since when have I cared about public opinion?" Floyd retorted.

"Since when has the public cared about you?" the chief interjected. "The rules are changing."

"That's what I keep telling him," Adams said. "Floyd, try to understand. This is a game of politics. Let the politicians handle it."

"No," Floyd said flatly. "I have to keep working on this. You can refuse to help me, but I can't stop working."

"We're trying to protect you!" Adams exclaimed.

"That's sweet," Floyd said sarcastically, "Considering *I'm* supposed to be the protector!"

"Even you need a little help sometime," the chief said mildly.

"Please listen to us," Adams pleaded. "Step away from your ego for just a minute and recognize that we're right."

"No," Floyd shook his head. "I'm not backing away from this. You want to talk about dangerous? What's dangerous is giving them any kind of power over this city. It has to be stopped now."

"They don't care about the city," Adams protested. "They want you. Isn't that what Kelly said?"

"So they want me dead," Floyd said. "Why do you suppose that is? So that they can take over the city. And if I disappear they won't care about me anymore. They'll still take over the city. And I swear that's not going to happen. Not on my watch."

"There's more at stake here than just the city," the chief said. "Don't be a fool, Floyd."

"It's too late for that," Floyd said tersely. "Now, if you'll excuse me, I have a supervillain coalition to take down."

He turned and stalked out of the office.

....

Four hours, several drinks, and two brawls later found Floyd sitting on a rooftop staring out at the city in a mood that became increasingly despondent. It looked much simpler from up high. The world seemed peaceful and small. People hurried about their business like ants in a busy hive, with no idea that their lives depended on Floyd's decision.

He knew he couldn't sit up there indefinitely, as tempting as it was. Getting kicked out of Scotland Yard was the final straw, the kick he needed to get out and do something. And the only thing he knew to do was to go out and meet the villains on their terms, and offer them the one thing he knew they wanted. It was four o'clock in the morning when he let himself into Kelly's basement again.

"Not you again," Kelly groaned. "What do you want?"

"I need to get a message to Rex King Cobra and all his associates," Floyd said, helping himself to a chair. "Can you do that?"

"I can do that in my sleep," the hacker scoffed. "What's the catch?"

"No catch," Floyd said. "I'm just not as good at this stuff as I'd like to be. And preferably, I'd like the entire world to hear the message."

"Ah, so you want me to hack into like... all the radio and TV, too?" Kelly scoffed. "Why didn't you say so in the first place?"

Floyd frowned. "I thought I did."

"Fine," Kelly grumbled. "Give me ten minutes. Is this police business, too?"

"This is world-saving business," Floyd said. "The police bailed out on me."

"That's why you don't get mixed up with the authorities," Kelly said wisely. "You should know better."

"Don't give me advice," Floyd snapped. "Have you got it ready?"

"Yeah, yeah," the kid said, handing him a pair of headphones. "We are live, world-wide in five, four, three, two..."

He raised one finger silently and nodded at Floyd.

"This message is for the Supervillains of London. You have told the citizens of Earth that you come in peace. This is a lie. You have said that you have no intentions of murder or mayhem. This is a lie. You have said that I am a threat to your existence, and that is the one thing you have said that is true."

He took a deep breath and continued.

"My name is Jeffry Lewis Floyd. This city and this planet are under my protection. I will not let you take it by force or by guile. If you truly wish to eliminate the threat I pose to you, then come to me directly and meet me on my terms. I will be waiting for you on the Tower Bridge, tonight, at 6 PM. Do not make me come find you."

He signaled to Kelly, who quickly switched off the stream. His mouth had fallen open in amazement.

"That was an insanely stupid thing to do," he commented finally.

"I know," Floyd retorted. "Let's hope they think so, too."

COMPUTER FILE 5.8.1
Battlefield

Whenever possible, choose your own battlefield. The one who chooses the battlefield has the advantage and the one with the advantage has the greater chance of success. You have a very good head for heights; high buildings and bridges will be the best locations. You're small and lithe and many structures that support you will collapse under a heavier opponent.

Super strength is one of the most common attributes among supervillains, and you will never be their equal physically. Let gravity do your work for you. A fall from a decent height will kill most and incapacitate others for several minutes. It will also kill or incapacitate you so it goes without saying to watch your footing.

If you have the luxury of time, try to choose locations that are uninhabited. Warn local authorities to close off any structures you're planning to fight on. The less innocent people die in an encounter, the more favourably it will be viewed by the press.

A TIME TO SWEAR

Before supervillains, before Earth, Floyd had been happy.

He didn't realize at the time how incredibly fortunate an existence this was. He knew he was happy, but he didn't recognize the importance of this fact, or how fragile a state of being it was. He loved his work, he loved where he lived, and he spent his days drinking, singing, and dancing with the stars.

His sister called him "good for nothing" and perpetually threatened to throw him out. It was true that he couldn't hold down a job with any company in the city, preferring to do free lance work that allowed him "more creative freedom." It was this very creative freedom that, according to his sister, prevented him from actually getting any freelance work. But Floyd didn't care.

The most pain he'd ever been in was when he broke his leg jumping from the top of the nineteenth spire just to prove he could.

"You only proved you couldn't," his sister had pointed out, narrowing her eyes, and Floyd had stopped swearing long enough to laugh and say that she'd completely missed the point.

When his sister had announced her engagement, Floyd had been happy for them both. Her fiancee had behaved remarkably coolly towards his future brother-in-law when they were introduced. He was a successful businessman with money and class.

"We're going to sell the house," his sister told him. "We won't be living here."

"That's great," Floyd had responded. They hadn't said anything.

"I'm coming with, right?" Floyd had asked, a flicker of unease running across his face. They looked at each other, and he looked between them.

"Right?" he repeated.

He had gone out celebrating the next night and come home drunk, and singing at the top of his lungs. His future brother-in-law opened the door without a word, his face as long as an undertaker's.

"You're going to be happy," Floyd told him generously, staggering towards the kitchen.

"I saved you supper," his sister said with uncharacteristic gentleness. Floyd was delighted and grateful and ebullient. He found out later that she'd laced the food with a drug provided by the Department of Supervillain Help and Relief Services. Toasting them both and wishing them joy and happiness was the last thing he remembered before his world turned to hell.

....

She walked softly through his dreams, banishing the shadows by her presence. She knelt beside him and her touch was like a whisper, but it called him out of the dreamworld and back to the nightmare of reality. Floyd awoke in the darkness to discover he was no longer alone.

Her presence startled him, and he tried to ask her name, but he choked on the inquiry, and she pressed a finger to his lips.

"Don't try to talk," she said softly. "Everything's going to be all right."

He could see her through the glimmer of death in his eyes, and she was beautiful. Raven black hair fell past her waist, framing a face both delicate and seductive. There was something familiar about her that he could not place, something that called to him through the thick fog of exhaustion and made him want to impress her.

"Who are you?" he whispered, in spite of her admonishment.

She smiled enigmatically. "I am your darkest fears," she answered, "and your deepest desires."

He frowned, and tried to figure out what it meant, but there was too much confusion.

"I'm dying," he said, stating the obvious. He stared into her eyes, wishing he could find solace there, but she was a stranger to him.

"It doesn't have to be this way," she offered. "You've seen my power. I can take you home again, Floyd."

He knew who she was. He felt surprisingly indifferent about the realization.

"Telepath."

She smiled when he spoke her name.

"Do you remember my offer?" she asked. "I can make the nightmares go away. I can set you free."

He tried desperately to remember what was at stake, but he had already lost everything. He knew the right answer was no, but he didn't know why. He didn't have the strength to keep fighting for something he had never believed in the first place.

"I can take you home," she promised, holding our her hand. "Back to when you were happy, and things were perfect... all you have to do is accept it."

"I want this to be over," he said, pleading with his eyes, begging for acceptance. "I don't want to be alone anymore."

She smiled; her expression full of sadness, pity, and triumph. "You will never be alone again," she promised.

Floyd paused to consider. Every breath sent stabbing pains through his chest. Every heartbeat was slowing towards his last. There was no one to mount a rescue, and no one to miss him when he was gone. The nanobots would do their best to knit him back together, but they had nothing to work with. They ran off the same energy that kept his blood beating, and it was quickly running out. Their attempts would simply kill him faster.

"I'll lose the game," he said finally.

"You never stood a chance at winning," the villainess told him. "And it ends the same way regardless."

"Are you really her?" he asked. "I never expected you to be..."

"Beautiful?" She smiled. "The world is full of surprises, Floyd."

He shivered when she said his name. He wanted to accept her offer, wanted to be with her, more than anything he could remember wanting before. And what did it matter if he died anyway?

Slowly, he slipped his hand into hers.

"Swear to me," she whispered. "Your undying loyalty."

He swallowed. "I swear."

"Swear to me," she said again. "Your unending devotion."

It became easier with repetition. "I swear."

"Swear to be mine," she finished, "until the day you die."

The man who was already as good as dead thought he was giving away nothing as he answered.

"I swear."

She closed her fingers around his hand, and the darkness dissolved into bliss.

WAR ON SUPERVILLAINS ESCALATES
September 26, 2013

Early this morning, a yet-unidentified hacker was able to broadcast a message intended for London, but including the entire world. In the message a man identifying himself as Jeffry Lewis Floyd challenged the superhumans whom he styles "Supervillains of London" to destroy him themselves if he poses such a threat.

While the demand was issued directly at the superhumans now claiming British citizenship, the entire planet was included in the broadcast. The hacker who may or may not actually be the vigilante the superhumans wish to be taken into custody claimed to have the entire planet under custody.

The showdown is scheduled to take place on the Tower Bridge at 6 PM tonight. People are warned to stay away from the area as authorities attempt to take the suspect into custody. It is extremely unlikely that any battle will occur, and the peaceful intentions of the superhumans has been made abundantly clear. However, the suspect may be armed and dangerous.

A TIME TO FIGHT

Adams didn't expect to see Floyd again. He'd declined to be a part of the posse sent to arrest Floyd when he appeared on the Tower Bridge. Instead he went home and waited—for what, he didn't know. He watched the news, which reported on the superhumans rights movement, promised live footage of the stand-off on the bridge, and talked about the weather, which was rainy.

The knock on the door came at four in the afternoon. He ignored it at first, assuming it was just the postman, but it persisted. Finally, he slid back the bolt and opened the door on the pouring rain, and the bedraggled figure who stood drenched in it.

"Floyd," he said, not sure what else to say. "What are you doing at my house?" he demanded.

"You know," Floyd said, walking past him into the house, "whenever I ask you that question, you never answer. So I'm not going to answer either."

Adams shut the door behind him.

"They're waiting for you," he said. "They're going to arrest you if you show up on that bridge."

"Yeah, I know," Floyd said. "That's why I'm here. I need your help."

"I can't help you with this," Adams said. "Just don't show up. That's what they're expecting anyway."

Floyd shook his head. "I can't do that," he said. "I issued a challenge, and I have to be there."

"No you don't," Adams said fervently. "This is madness, Floyd."

"It's the only way," Floyd said. "Please, help me. I can't go against the police unarmed."

"You're not going against the police, armed or not," Adams said severely. "Stay."

Floyd stood unmoving for the thirty seconds it took Adams to fetch a towel.

"You're dripping all over the carpet," he complained. "What are you doing here?"

"I'm sorry," Floyd said softly. "I shouldn't have come. I don't know what I was thinking."

"If you go to that bridge, you're going to be arrested, or outlawed, or killed," Adams said. "You can't possibly win. You probably won't even see a supervillain."

"I have to try," Floyd said. "You know I have to try."

"Floyd..." Adams raised his hands and dropped them helplessly. "I do," he admitted. "I do know that. I just wish you would listen to me for once."

Floyd looked pained, but he didn't answer.

"I can't do anything for you, Floyd," Adams said formally.

"I know," Floyd repeated. "I know. I'm not asking you to get involved. It's just... I need weapons. I can talk my way past the police, but I have to have something to face the supervillains with."

"I can't do that, Floyd."

"Do you have any idea how long I'll last out there unarmed?" Floyd pleaded. "I can take down a few, but I can never win against them all. I know you keep all the weapons you keep confiscating from me. I need access."

"No," Adams said.

Floyd opened his mouth to protest and shut it again. "No, of course not," he said. "You're right. I have no right to march in here and demand that of you—you can't break your oath. You have a duty too, and I—"

He turned to go, and for inexplicable reasons, Adams suddenly felt guilty.

"Floyd, wait," he said. Floyd stopped but didn't turn.

"I'm sorry," Adams said lamely.

"Don't mention it," Floyd said shortly.

For a moment, Adams almost let him go.

"No, wait," he said, grasping his shoulder. "I mean it. I really am sorry. I was so focused on *appearing* to do the right thing that I forgot what was most important..."

He trailed off at the look of confusion on Floyd's face.

"Forget it," he said. "I forgot that the concepts of right and wrong elude you."

"Is that an insult?" Floyd asked.

Adams rolled his eyes.

"Well is it?" Floyd demanded. "It's entirely possible I'm going to die tonight, and if that's the case I'd rather that the last thing I hear from you not be..."

"Don't say that," Adams said firmly. "You're going to beat these guys. I've seen you in worse situations."

"Well I haven't," Floyd muttered. "I don't know anything about them—what they've got, what their plans are..."

He lost his mask, and his eyes reflected his fear. "They're coming for *me*," he said softly. "What does that mean?"

"It's not too late to pull back and make an intelligent plan first," Adams said. "Do some reconnaissance. Don't go rushing into things headlong with no idea what you're getting into."

Floyd shook his head. "There isn't time," he said. "I wish you could understand... I can't let them get a foothold. I can't let them think I'm afraid of them."

"Do you really think they're going to come to the bridge tonight?" Adams asked.

"They're supervillains," Floyd said with confidence. "They'll come."

Adams paused in consideration, and then sighed. He crossed the room, opened a desk drawer, reached into the back and pulled out a key.

"Here." He handed it to Floyd. "This opens the storage facility where we store all the tech we've been confiscating from supervillains for the last six months."

Floyd stared at it uncertainly. "Joseph, if they found out you gave this to me..."

"Don't," Adams interrupted. "If you don't win this fight it doesn't matter what they do or do not find out about me."

"Thank you," Floyd said. He seemed about to say something else, but changed his mind. "Thank you," he repeated.

"Just be careful," Adams begged.

"That word's not in my vocabulary," Floyd said with a grin. "You know that."

"Good luck then," Adams said,. "You're going to need it."

Floyd nodded briefly, and then he opened the door and stepped back out into the pouring rain.

....

The bridge was surrounded by cars with flashing lights, and men in uniform and grim faces. Floyd walked up to them slowly, not wanting to spark off any altercation.

The chief inspector stood at the gate to the bridge, blocking his way.

"Drop your weapons," he said calmly, "And put your hands on your head."

"I can't do that," Floyd said.

"I am ordering you—" the chief said slowly.

"I not here to fight you," Floyd interrupted. "I'm here to stop the monsters that want to destroy your city."

His eyes dared anyone to contradict him. No one did.

"I'm the only one who can stop them," he said. "You know that."

He glanced around to include all the policemen present. "You *all* know that," he repeated. "These supervillains don't come in peace."

The chief inspector's resolve wavered only for a minute, and then returned. "I have my orders," he said firmly.

"Fine," Floyd said. "Follow your orders. You don't want a situation here, after all, I'm just an insane lunatic. If the supervillains do not answer my challenge, then I will come down and surrender to you at dawn."

"How do I know you aren't lying?" the chief inspector asked.

"Look in my eyes," Floyd said. "I have never lied to you and I'm not lying now. If the supervillains do not answer my summons then I will surrender to you at dawn. No one needs to get hurt."

"And if they do?"

"If they do?" Floyd repeated. "If they do," he laughed, "You can come collect the bodies."

"Including yours?" asked the chief inspector.

"Probably," Floyd said with a smile.

The chief inspector sighed and stepped aside. "The bridge is yours," he said formally. "Until dawn."

"Thank you," Floyd said, stepping past him. He paused before crossing the gate, and glanced at the assembled faces.

"You could come with me," he said to the Metropolitan Police Force. "You could help me fight."

No one stirred.

Alone, Floyd stepped onto the bridge.

....

The rain had finally stopped, but Floyd shivered as he paced the length of the Tower

Bridge. The sun was setting, and the storm clouds parted to reveal a brilliant glimpse of orange and red streaked sky. Floyd paused and leaned on the railing to watch. He didn't hear the disturbance at the gate behind him, didn't look up from his reverie until someone tapped him on the shoulder.

He whirled around instantly, prepared to fight, but there was no supervillain in sight.

"It's me," Adams said, taking an instinctive step backwards. "If it wasn't me, you'd be a dead man."

Floyd let out his breath, closing his eyes briefly in an attempt to relax.

"What are you doing here?" he said finally. "You could get killed."

"That didn't stop you," Adams pointed out. He gestured, and Floyd saw the police ranged behind him on Floyd's side of the guard-bridge. "I brought reinforcements."

"You brought reinforcements?" Floyd said incredulously.

"They're volunteers," Adams said. "We figured that if you lose this fight, we won't even have a career to worry about."

Floyd stared at his friend's face and had nothing to say.

"You need them," Adams said. "If for nothing else then to stand guard for you. Anyone could have snuck up here."

Floyd sighed. "I'm just tense," he said. "I was watching the sunset and—"

His shoulders rose and fell in a gesture of defeat. "I wish I could tell you to go home, that I have this under control," he said. "But I'm afraid that I don't understand anything anymore."

"We've got your back," Adams promised, touching his shoulder briefly. "We've got a city to save."

The sun dipped below the horizon, leaving the city lights to glitter against a black sky. Adams shoved his hands deep into his coat pocket and turned to look over the river.

"London is beautiful at night," he commented. Floyd didn't answer, unwilling to admit how much the city affected him and equally reluctant to make light of something so serious.

The night dragged on. Helicopters broadcasting live footage of the stand-off wheeled off to report on more interesting events. People in their homes changed the channel to the latest political debate.

"Will they come?" Adams asked Floyd.

"They'll come," Floyd said. "They have to."

"If they don't," Adams asked, "What will you do then?"

Floyd didn't answer. "They have to come," he repeated.

"Tell me honestly," Adams asked, searching his face. "Can you win this fight?"

Floyd stared at a point beyond his shoulder and swore.

"They're here," he said softly. Adams looked and saw nothing but darkness.

"What do we do?" he asked.

"You read my blog," Floyd said, starting towards the end of the bridge. "Kill them."

EPILOGUE

Once upon a time there was a young man who lived on the most beautiful planet in the world. He had lost his parents when he was very young, and his sister had got all the responsibility of raising him. She detested the job, and never hesitated to make her dislike known, but it never troubled the young man. He ran with bad company and drank the nights away, and danced among the stars with the most beautiful woman in the world.

They sat together on a bridge that stretched like spiders-web between two towers, under the twinkling stars of an unending night. The dark haired girl slipped her fingers through the young man's hand, and smiled at him. He drank in the expression in adoration, ignoring the unsettling feeling her gaze always raised in him.

"Do you love me?" she asked frankly.

"More than anything in the world," he confessed.

"Tell me a story," the dark-haired girl demanded. "Tell me about this city."

He didn't question her lack of knowledge, and he acquiesced to her wishes as always. He searched his mind for the perfect story; one that was important to him as well as intriguing to her.

"During the... the seventeenth dynasty, I think..." he began slowly, "There was a war. A free-thinking band of radicals calling themselves the *shamry-hadar* marched on the City of a Thousand Spires. They said they were going to destroy it."

"And what happened?"

"Well, the army came, and when they reached the city... it was empty. There were no armies to face them, no defenses; nothing. Instead, all the people had gone inside, locked their doors and barred the windows. So when the rebels arrived they found the streets empty.

"And... and it was silent. They'd shut off anything that made noise, and the legend has it that as the army walked through the streets gradually they stopped chanting. They stopped challenging and threatening, and they listened.

"And huddling in their homes in fear, the inhabitants of the city also listened. And everything was still."

The young man paused, listening to the stillness of the stars that surrounded him, and somewhere in that darkness his heart cried, even when his mind could not remember why.

"They say that when the city is quiet, when the people are silent and still... they say that all you can hear is the wind singing through the spires. And they say... they say that the singing will drive you mad. They say that, when it's that quiet, that it's not the wind any more—it's the stars. And that the starsong isn't meant to be heard by mortal ears."

He turned to look at the girl, to see if she'd enjoyed the story, but she wasn't there anymore. He was alone. The knowledge drove fear into his heart. He scrambled to his feet, looking for her, but there was no sign of where she had gone.

Suddenly the bridge tilted beneath his feet. He struggled to hold on, but the ropes came apart between his fingers and he was falling; falling through the glittering city, through the star-spangled sky, through darkness, through reality. Falling until he landing on a cold metal floor, and breathed the damp air, and tasted blood on his tongue and gradually understood that he had never been on that bridge at all, that it was just a dream. A gorgeous dream. And now it was over.

The four walls of his metal prison closed in around him, and there was no escape. He screamed for someone to hear him, and there was no answer. A steady ticking in his mind counted down the last minute of the three weeks he'd been given to live. He collapsed to his knees, sobbing, and realized he had never been awake to begin with.

Facts and answers and realizations whirled through his mind; a lifetime of questions and doubts and fears flashing before his eyes. One thought stood out among the others, like a shining sun-star rising above his city. One chilling thought as his breathing ceased, his heart stopped beating, and the nanobots in his system stopped fighting the battle they had already lost.

He had put his faith in a supervillain, and she had betrayed him.

To Be Continued...

Supervillains of London

Coming on October 6, 2013

Ev'ry seven years the faeries give
A tithe to Hell on All Hallows Eve
Now that they have me I do fear
That I will be the Teind this year

To report a supervillain
or learn more about the series,
visit:

supervillainoftheday.com

A NOTE ABOUT ENGLAND

Being an American writing about England is one of the most terrifying and exhilarating things I have ever done. I've done my best to be as accurate as possible when setting this series in London, but we're all human and can make mistakes. If you're an expert or a resident of England and you find an error in this narrative, be sure to let me know about it! I'll take the correction under consideration when writing future novels, and possibly even correct the error in the omnibus version.

Submit errors using the form provided on supervillainoftheday.com and you could earn yourself a copy of the ebook version of the next novel in the series!

ABOUT THE AUTHOR

Katie is a writer of many talents, constantly branching out into new fields and genres. She primarily writes novels and short stories in the science fiction and fantasy genres, along with an assortment of hilarious and sentimental poetry. When she's not writing she's acting, directing, singing, playing her Celtic harp or songwriting, often engaging in more than one at a time. She lives in the beautiful hills of Kentucky with her parents and eight siblings.

Visit her website at <u>katielynndaniels.com</u>

Or follow her on twitter @danielskatie